THEO'S NOT SO DIFFERENT

CISSY MOSELEY

Illustrated by Jane Luna

Acknowledgment

I'm grateful for many blessings, too many to number here. However, for this project, I want to thank my sister for encouraging me to write a children's book. She, a retired elementary school principal, can be very persuasive! And thanks to my daughter-in-law, Heather, who safely steered me through the unique language and daily culture of a classroom.

I am beyond thankful for my nephew Josh and niece Candace, who first opened their huge hearts and beautiful home to our buddy Case and now sweet baby Colt. Our family has been delightfully changed forever.

A shout out to my friend Michele, who patiently answered my questions and gave me the image of "hearts being stitched together through love." You, Scott, your beautiful children—Patrick, Ellee, and Abigail—and other families like yours broaden our hearts and minds to see possibilities where none seemed to exist.

I'm thankful for each birth mother who seeks a safe and loving home for her baby through adoption, which is ALWAYS a choice.

Finally, I'm thankful for my built-in focus group—my husband, my grandchildren, and their parents—who graciously gathered on the back porch for an impromptu reading and gave excellent feedback. As always, they are my greatest blessings.

AuthorHouse™
1663 Liberty Drive
Bloomington, IN 47403
www.authorhouse.com
Phone: 833-262-8899

Because of the dynamic nature of the Internet, any web addresses or links contained in this book may have changed
since publication and may no longer be valid. The views expressed in this work are solely those of the author and do not
necessarily reflect the views of the publisher, and the publisher hereby disclaims any responsibility for them.

Any people depicted in stock imagery provided by Getty Images are models,
and such images are being used for illustrative purposes only.
Certain stock imagery © Getty Images.

This book is printed on acid-free paper.

ISBN: 978-1-7283-7863-3 (sc)
ISBN: 978-1-7283-7864-0 (hc)
ISBN: 978-1-7283-7862-6 (e)

Library of Congress Control Number: 2023901684

Print information available on the last page.

Published by AuthorHouse 02/10/2023

authorHOUSE

For Case and Colt

And for **everyone** who has struggled with
feeling different, **whatever the reason.**
Only love, not looks, can permanently
stitch our hearts together.

Theo's Not So Different

Theo is a cheerful boy who meets each day with an enthusiastic burst typical of most healthy, happy boys. He thinks his mama and daddy are the best! He loves when they take him camping, fishing, and swimming. He loves that they never miss his soccer or baseball games. Most of all, Theo loves to go to church with his family.

Mama cooks all his favorite foods. She takes pictures of everything Theo does. She has hundreds of photos—on the desk, walls, and shelves.

Lately, though, the pictures have been making Theo feel sad. Daddy noticed something was bothering Theo, and he asked, "What's wrong, buddy?" Theo sighed, "Daddy, why am I different? All my cousins look like their parents. My friends at church and soccer all look like their parents."

Theo grabbed his mama and daddy's hands and dragged them to the mirror. "Just look at me! Why am I different?" Together, they studied the mirror.

Mama and Daddy sat down in the big red chair and drew Theo close in their laps to snuggle. "Theo," Daddy said, "you know you're adopted, right?" "Yes," Theo said, "but I don't know what adopted means."

"Adoption is when a mom and dad love a child so much that they choose him to be a part of their family. You don't look like us on the outside, but love stitched our hearts together the first moment we saw you. The awesome truth is that because we adopted you this is your home, and you will be our little boy forever and ever."

That night when they knelt for bedtime prayers, Daddy thanked God for sending Theo to be their son. Theo prayed, "Thank you, God, for Mama and Daddy, who will love me forever and ever. But, please, God, send me friends who look like me."

Mama held Theo's small hand while Daddy said, "Son, God makes each of us different but also the same. That means we can look different but feel the same inside our hearts. Remember, it's far better to share friendships and treat people kindly than notice how different they look.

Walking away from Theo's room, Mama asked with a heavy heart, "Do you think he will understand and not be sad?" Daddy hugged her tenderly and said, "We will always pray for our boy to be happy." Every night after that, Theo prayed for friends like him, and Mama and Daddy prayed for their boy to be happy.

On the first day of school, Theo threw back his favorite blanket and jumped out of bed. He was bright-eyed and so excited! He could hardly wait to start the day because his heart knew God would send him new friends who were just like him.

As Mama walked Theo to the school's front door, an energetic boy bounced a soccer ball right to Theo. He swiped his hair from his laughing brown eyes and said, "Hi, I'm Noah, and I play soccer!" Theo caught the ball and said, "Hey, I play soccer too. You're just like me!"

Noah smiled brilliantly, saying, "That's so cool. Let's be friends!" Without another word, shoulder to shoulder, Theo and Noah entered the school together.

When it was time to switch morning groups, Theo saw a friendly boy with brownish-blond hair at the science station. He waved Theo over and said, "Hey, I'm Xander, and I want to be a scientist!" Theo's beaming smile brightened even more, and he said, "I love science. You're just like me!"

Together, Xander and Theo examined life through a microscope and found it AMAZING.

18

As the day passed, Theo met more classmates. During morning recess, he was surprised when Aki did a backflip on the sidewalk. Theo jumped up in her pathway, saying, "Whoa! Awesome! Do you take gymnastics?" Aki answered, "Yes, I compete with other girls my age." Theo said, "That's so cool! I want to learn gymnastics. Will you show me?"

Aki took the time to show Theo a simple cartwheel. Theo tried but fell right at Aki's feet. Laughing as he picked himself up, he said, "I think I need more practice!" Aki agreed to help him a little each day.

At lunchtime, Ryan suddenly ran up to the other children with a bat and ball. Theo pumped his fist in the air as he whooped, "BASEBALL!?! I LOVE baseball!! You're just like me! Can we play right now?"

Ryan agreed, saying, "I hoped you would play with me." Aki and Noah leaped up and quickly said, "YEAH, count us in!" So, Ryan, Aki, Noah, and Theo played ball until lunch ended.

At afternoon recess, from across the playground, Theo spied Liam playing in the sandbox with tractors and construction trucks. Theo hustled to the sandbox and asked, "Do YOU like tractors?" Liam, covered with sand from head to toe, exclaimed, "OH, I LOVE TRACTORS AND TRUCKS!" Theo tumbled right into the sandbox on the road Liam built and declared, "Me too! Me too! YOU'RE JUST LIKE ME!"

Theo and Liam had fun talking about different kinds of tractors and trucks. They discovered Theo loved farm tractors and monster trucks, while Liam preferred construction trucks and heavy equipment.

They also discovered it was okay to have different opinions.

When recess ended, Theo asked Liam, "Will you race me back?" Liam ran off in a flash, calling, "Bet I beat you!" They laughed all the way to the classroom.

Later, when the teacher instructed the class to get their afternoon snacks, Theo noticed Malie had the same fruit crisps he had brought for a snack. He rushed to her side and exclaimed, "Hey, that is my favorite snack! See, I have it too. YOU'RE JUST LIKE ME!"

Malie laughed, "Yes, we ARE the same!" Theo said, "We are the same AND different! You laugh more than I do. I like your laugh."

Together, they ate their snacks, and Theo was fascinated to hear Malie was born in Hawaii and had just recently moved. He said, "I saw pictures of Hawaii, and I really want to go there!"

Theo added, "You know what, Malie? I like your name too!" She said, "Thanks. It's Hawaiian and means calm and brave."

Theo helped Malie tidy the lunch table, and he walked beside her as she wheeled herself back to her table.

Theo's first day passed so quickly that he never considered looking different. He was so happy that he dashed out the door into his parents' arms and proclaimed, "I LOVE SCHOOL!"

Mama and Daddy heard the happiness in Theo's voice, and it filled their hearts with joy.

On the drive home, Mama asked Theo, "Hey, Buddy, did you have a good day? Did you meet any friends like you?"

Scratching his head with a puzzled look, Theo answered, "They didn't LOOK like me, but they WERE like me.

Noah loves soccer, and he wants to be my friend.

Xander loves science. We shared a microscope.

Aki is a gymnast and wants to teach me to do a cartwheel.

Ryan loves baseball. He played with us at recess.

Liam loves tractors and trucks. Together, we built a road in the sandbox.

And I met a girl from Hawaii named Malie. She laughed a lot and brought fruit crisps for snacks, just like me!"

Then, a remarkable thing happened! A huge understanding smile spread slowly across Theo's face, and he whispered, "I guess I'm not so different after all because . . .."

Theo paused as he concluded, "THEY'RE ALL JUST LIKE ME!!"

From that day forward, they all searched for each other's similarities and overlooked their differences. Together, they learned and loved more each day!

CPSIA information can be obtained
at www.ICGtesting.com
Printed in the USA
LVHW071947170323
741893LV00008B/478